I think you'll agree,
he's a little bit funny-looking.

To say the least.

He lives in a world of cute, fluffy things.

OFFICIAL PILE
OF
EXTREME
CUTENESS

LoVe MOnSteR

Rachel Bright

WELCOME TO
CUTESVILLE
Home of the fluffy

HarperCollins Children's Books

This
is a mOnster.

(Hello, Monster.)

which makes being
funny-looking...

pretty,

darn

hard.

You might have noticed that **everybody loves**

kittens...

and puppies...

and bunnies.

You know,
cute, fluffy
things.

But **nObOdy lOves**
a slightly **hairy,**
I-suppose-a-bit-gOOgly-eyed
mOnster.

(POor Monster.)

This might be enough to make a monster
feel, well, a bit down in the dumps.
But not being the moping-around sort,

he decided to
set out and look
for someone who'd
love him,
just the way he was.

He looked high.

He looked low.

tumbleweed

And Out.

More than once he thought that maybe...

just maybe...

he'd found what he was looking for.

But, as it turned out, things were
never quite as they seemed.

Yes, it would be
fair to say
that his search
did **not** go well.

And then it didn't
go well some more.

It didn't go well for
such a long time, in fact,

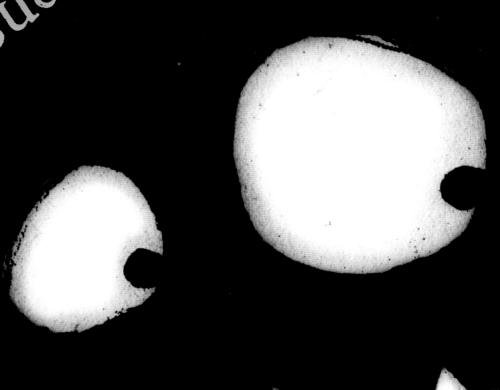

that it began to get

dark.

And
scary.

And, well,

not very nice.

So the monster,
having lost all his umpf,
decided it was time to give up.

BUS TO CUTESVILLE

and go hOme.

But in the blink of a **gOo**gly eye...

everything
Changed.

You see,
Sometimes,
when you least expect it...

love
finds you.

For the monsters who've found me
(& one slightly hairy one in particular)

WELCOME TO CUTESVILLE Home of the fluffy

and slighty hairy

PAINT

nails

And with Special
wow-you're-amazing thank-yous to Mandy,
Nancy, Helen, Ann-Janine, Kayt, James & Rose

First published in paperback in Great Britain by HarperCollins *Children's Books* in 2012
This edition published in 2020

10

ISBN: 978-0-00-744546-2

HarperCollins *Children's Books* is a division of HarperCollins*Publishers* Ltd.

Text and illustrations copyright © Rachel Bright 2012

The author/illustrator asserts the moral right to be identified as the author/illustrator of the work.
A CIP catalogue record for this title is available from the British Library. All rights reserved.

HarperCollinsPublishers 1st Floor, Watermarque Building, Ringsend Road Dublin 4, Ireland

Visit our website at: www.harpercollins.co.uk

Printed and bound in China